Silly Snowmen

Coloring Book

John Kurtz

Dover Publications, Inc.
Mineola, New York

Inside this fun and fanciful coloring book, you will find thirty illustrations of snowmen and their reindeer friends doing all sorts of silly things. Go along with them as they barbecue carrots in the snow, hang out at the beach, and have other wild adventures. All you need are crayons, markers, or colored pencils to join in on the fun.

Bibliographical Note

Silly Snowmen Coloring Book is a new work, first published by Dover Publications, Inc., in 2015.

International Standard Book Number

ISBN-13: 978-0-486-79743-4
ISBN-10: 0-486-79743-0

Manufactured in the United States by RR Donnelley
79743001 2015
www.doverpublications.com

SNOW
MAN!